SEE HOW THEY GROW

LAMB

photographed by
G O R D O N   C L A Y T O N

Lodestar Books • Dutton • New York

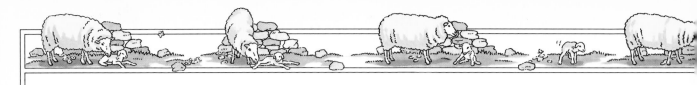

Just born

I am just four
hours old. I can
see and hear, but
my legs are very
weak. They wobble
and shake.

I am hungry.
I drink my mother's
milk. My sister wants
to feed too.

Now I am tired.
My woolly coat will
keep me warm
while I sleep.

Getting stronger

I am one day old. My legs are
getting stronger. I keep very
close to my mother and bleat
loudly when she goes away.

8

I can only stand
for a short time
before I fall down.

But I soon
get up again.

Exploring

I am one week old. My sister
and I are growing up fast.

I am interested in
everything I see and hear.
There's a new bale of straw.
I wonder what it's like.

Mmm, the straw smells nice,
but it tickles my nose!

11

Growing up

I am four weeks old now. My woolly
coat is growing thicker.

I love to run
and play with
my sister. Shall
we jump over
these logs?

13

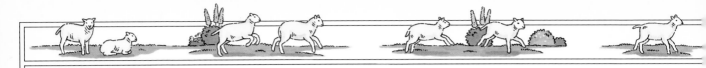

Playing together

Now I am eight weeks old. I like to chase
my sister and the other lambs
around the field.

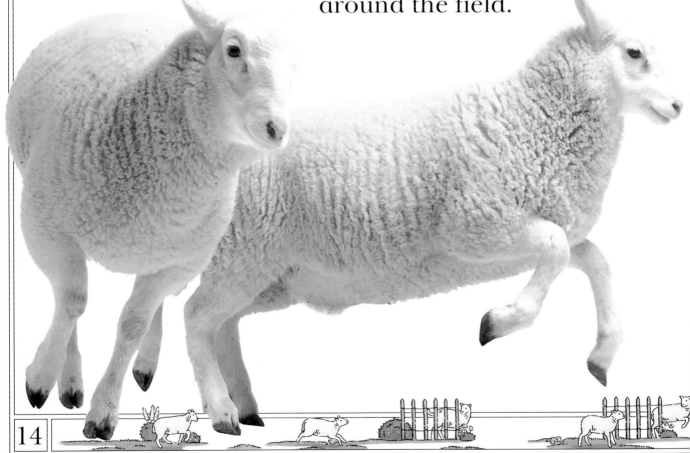

14

Where is
my sister?

Here she is. She nuzzles my face.

Nibbling the grass

I am ten weeks old.
I nibble the grass and love
the fresh grass best.

My sister and I
often graze together.
We hardly ever feed
from our mother.

Grass is very tough
to chew. So I chew it
over and over again
until it is soft.

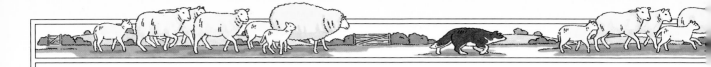

Nearly grown up

I am twelve weeks old. My sister
and I spend most of the day grazing
with the older sheep.

Our wool is growing longer.
We are nearly as big as our mother.
Soon we will be fully grown.

See how I grew

Four hours old   One day old

One week old   Four weeks old   Eight weeks old

Ten weeks old   Twelve weeks old